THE CINDER-EYED CATS

THE CINDER-EYED CATS

ERIC ROHMANN

DRAGONFLY BOOKS NEW YORK

In faraway lands,

When twilight falls on fair and wind-swept days,

Cats like velvet shadows move,

Their coal-fire eyes ablaze.

And on those bright and moonlit nights while all the world's asleep,

Creatures wake beneath the waves and rise up from the deep.

The moonlight whirls, the stars burst out,
The sand and wind and ocean sway,
And from the grip of earth and sea,
The creatures make their getaway.

Throughout the night the tunas twirl, the starfish weave and wiggle,
And as the sardines dance, their shiny brine-filled bellies jiggle.

Growls and laughter echo in the deepest dark of night,
And fishes round the fire spark like cats' eyes in the light.

Then a flash of early morning sun, the waking light of dawn,
Calls the creatures to the sea,

And suddenly they're gone.

Quiet now the sea-blue sky, no dancing on the shore—

Until the twilight falls again

And the moon comes round once more.

Published by
Dragonfly Books
an imprint of
Random House Children's Books
a division of Random House, Inc.
1540 Broadway
New York, New York 10036

Visit us on the Web! www.randomhouse.com/kids

Educators and librarians, for a variety of teaching tools, visit us at
www.randomhouse.com/teachers

Library of Congress Cataloging-in-Publication Data

Rohmann, Eric.
The cinder-eyed cats / Eric Rohmann.
p. cm.
Summary: A boy makes a magical trip to a tropical island where he and five cinder-eyed cats watch as various sea creatures emerge from the ocean to dance by their campfire.
[1. Night—Fiction. 2. Marine animals—Fiction. 3. Cats—Fiction. 4. Stories in rhyme.]
1. Title
ISBN: 0-517-70896-5 (trade)
       0-517-70897-3 (lib. bdg.)
       0-440-41743-0 (pbk.)
PZ7.R6413Ci 1997
[E]—dc21
97-6763

Reprinted by arrangement with Crown Publishers

Printed in the United States of America
November 2001

10 9 8 7 6 5 4 3 2 1